Please return/renew this item by the
last date shown to avoid a charge.
Books may also be renewed by phone
and Internet. May not be renewed if
required by another reader.

www.libraries.barnet.gov.uk

LONDON BOROUGH

Special thanks to Tabitha Jones
For Leo Loveridge

ORCHARD BOOKS

First published in Great Britain in 2018 by The Watts Publishing Group

1 3 5 7 9 10 8 6 4 2

Text © 2018 Beast Quest Limited
Cover and inside illustrations by Dynamo
© Beast Quest Limited 2018

Team Hero is a registered trademark in the European Union
Series created by Beast Quest Limited, London

A CIP catalogue record for this book is available from the British Library.

ISBN 978 1 40835 197 0

Printed in Great Britain

MIX
Paper from
responsible sources
FSC® C104740

The paper and board used in this book are made from wood from responsible sources.

Orchard Books
An imprint of Hachette Children's Group
Part of The Watts Publishing Group Limited
Carmelite House, 50 Victoria Embankment, London EC4Y 0DZ

An Hachette UK Company
www.hachette.co.uk
www.hachettechildrens.co.uk

THE ICE WOLVES

ADAM BLADE

ORCHARD

MEET TEAM HERO ...

JACK

POWER: Super-strength

LIKES: Ventura City FC

DISLIKES: Bullies

RUBY

POWER: Fire vision
LIKES: Comic books
DISLIKES: Small spaces

DANNY

POWER: Super-hearing, able to generate sonic blasts
LIKES: Pizza
DISLIKES: Thunder

CONTENTS

CHANCELLOR REX sat at his desk waiting for Commandant Eckles to respond. The tall, straight-backed leader of the Hightower Legion stood with her back to him, gazing out through the high arched window that overlooked Hero Academy. Despite being almost as old as Rex himself, she had the build and bearing of a soldier at her peak. Her armour shone and her blonde hair was cropped.

"Are you sure you won't take a seat?" Rex asked.

Commandant Eckles turned, fixing him with cool grey eyes. "Whatever threat you may think you foresee," she said, "we can look after ourselves. Hightower Legion is the most skilled fighting force on the planet."

Rex closed his eyes, frustration building inside him. "You're not listening," he said. "Just because General Gore has been defeated, that doesn't mean the world is safe. The

High Command will stop at nothing to conquer the Earth's surface, and–"

"Look," Commandant Eckles said, cutting him off. "I hope I haven't travelled all the way from Mount Razor School to be lectured about the dangers that threaten the world. Remember, our founder, Wulfstan Hightower, was defeating evil long before your founder, Gretchen of Ventura, even knew which end of a sword to hold."

"A pity, then, that Wulfstan vanished just when the world needed him the most," Rex growled. But as soon as he saw anger flash across

Eckles's face, he regretted the words. He forced a weary smile. "Forgive me, Commandant," he said. "Hightower Legion and Team Hero are both sworn to defend our world from evil. We're on the same side. And I can't just sit by, knowing that the Legion is in danger."

Eckles arched an eyebrow. "As I said, we can look after ourselves."

"I hope so," Rex said. "But before deciding that — let me show you what I have seen." Rex lifted his hands, and a familiar rush of power washed through him as he activated his ability to project visions of the future. A rippling image like that from a

holographic projector formed in the
air. It showed a range of jagged, snow-
capped mountains spread beneath a
sky turned black with smoke. Huge
balls of fire streaked down through
the darkness, exploding where
they landed. Trees clinging to the
mountainside crackled with orange
flame. The vision zoomed in. Soldiers,
some of them children, stood in ragged
formation. Each bore the square tower
sigil of Wulfstan Hightower on their
battered armour. Their soot-blackened
faces were bruised and bloody, their
expressions grim. Most had lost their
weapons. Many were injured, and on

the scorched earth nearby lifeless bodies lay smouldering. All around them fire raged.

The vision faded. Commandant Eckles stood silent for a moment, her stern features still. "This is the future?" she asked.

Rex nodded. "Unless we work

together to prevent it. And in my
mind, the flames can mean only one
thing. The return of a very old enemy.
You know as well as I do, it will take
our combined forces to defeat her."

Eckles nodded slowly. "Then tell me,
Chancellor Rex." She narrowed her
eyes. "What do you propose?"

CHAPTER 1

MOUNTAIN ATTACK

"WAIT UP, guys!" Danny called.

Jack pulled his mule to a stop and looked back along the mountain path. *Not again!* For about the tenth time in as many minutes Danny was yanking at his trouser leg, trying to pull the frayed hem out of his mule's mouth. Ruby had her hands on her hips, watching him from her own mule.

"The stupid thing won't go!" Danny said, red-faced. "It just wants to eat my trousers!" He jabbed his heels into the creature's sides.

"Your mount isn't a thing," Ruby said. "She's a she. And of course she won't go if you keep kicking her! You've got to get on her good side."

"I don't think she's got a good side!" Danny said, pushing his sweaty black hair behind his bat-like ears. "I think she hates me."

"Nah," Ruby said, "if she hated you, she'd have dumped you off the mountain long ago."

Danny glanced over the edge of the mountain path, then anxiously back at his mule. The high, rocky path was so narrow the three Hero Academy students had to trot in single file. On one side, a sheer rock face stretched up towards the sky. To the other, the mountain dropped away so steeply it made Jack feel giddy to look down.

"Mules aren't like horses," Ruby said. "You can't boss them about. They have to want to carry you. Watch and learn, Danny boy." Ruby gave her mule's reins a gentle shake. Immediately, the creature started off at a smart trot.

Danny jerked his own mule's reins. The animal leapt forwards and Danny almost lurched out of the saddle. "Give me a hoverboard any day!" he muttered under his breath.

"Tell me about it," Jack said, as he set off in front of them. "We'd have reached Mount Razor days ago."

Jack heard a click in his earpiece as his Oracle, Hawk, activated. *"Hightower Legion doesn't permit the use of technology in the Shardmaw Mountains. I'm surprised they even permitted you to bring Oracles. The Legion believes using technology, like using special powers, is a weakness that does more harm than good."*

"They think superpowers are a weakness?" Jack said. Each of Jack's friends at Hero Academy had a special power. Danny had super-hearing, and could create sonic blasts with his voice. Ruby could shoot jets of fire from her eyes. Jack had once thought his scaly hands made him a freak, but since he'd been at Hero Academy, he'd come to rely on their supernatural strength. In fact, Jack had used his unique hands to help save the world more than once. Now the three friends had been sent by their headmaster, Chancellor Rex, on the first ever student exchange to Mount Razor School, where Hightower Legion students were trained. And from what Hawk said, it sounded like it would be about as much fun as a kick in the stomach.

"Correct," Hawk said. *"The Legion forbids the use of super powers."*

Listening to the conversation through her own Oracle, Ruby cut in. "But Wulfstan Hightower had super-strength himself! It doesn't make sense that they'd be against the use of special abilities, when their own founder was one of the most powerful heroes in history!"

"It would be most unwise to voice that opinion at Mount Razor," said Hawk. *"Even a thousand years on, the Legion still revere Wulfstan for his legendary skill and discipline.*  *They admire him because he honed his mind and body so he didn't need to rely on his super powers. The Legion keeps to his example as much as possible."*

"I don't understand why Chancellor Rex wants us to waste our time in some remote mountain base still stuck in the dark ages," muttered Danny.

Jack couldn't help agreeing. What could they possibly have to learn from the Legion?

The travellers rounded a sharp bend. "Whoa!" Jack pulled his mule to a sudden stop. The path ended in a pile of huge, grey boulders.

"There must have been a rockslide," Jack said, glancing up at the smooth cliff-face above them.

"Maybe we can climb over," Ruby said. But her mule shook its head and refused to budge.

"Danny, do you think you could shift

them with a sonic blast?" Jack asked.

Danny shrugged. "I'll give it a try."

He opened his mouth and let out a piercing shriek. Jack winced. A shudder ran through the rock-pile ahead. It shifted with a grating, groaning sound, but instead of rolling away, the rocks seemed to flow upwards. Jack watched, stunned, as the debris unfolded into the shape of a person.

The rock giant stood more than three metres tall on stocky, bowed legs. Fists like anvils hung at its sides. It rubbed its eyes, then snarled, baring tombstone teeth.

"It looks like some kind of rock ogre!" said Ruby, in awe.

"There's no match for this life form in my database," Hawk said. *"If you get*

closer, I can add it."

"Uh ... somehow, I think that would be a bad idea," Jack said. The rock creature growled, making Jack's insides vibrate.

"Maybe you're right," Hawk agreed. *"I detect animosity."* The rock ogre lurched forward, huge fists raised.

"I'll handle this," Ruby said. Two jets of flame shot from her eyes. They seared the air like blasts from twin blowtorches but they only glanced off the creature's shoulder, leaving a sooty smudge. "Or maybe not ..."

The ogre let out a bellow of rage almost as loud as Danny's sonic blast.

All three mules reared. Jack's stomach flipped as he flew from the saddle. He crashed to the ground, then flattened himself as Ruby's riderless mount leapt over him. Danny lay spreadeagled on the path, his mule following the two others down the mountain path.

"Run!" Ruby cried. They scrambled to their feet and sprinted away. Thunderous footsteps shook the mountainside as the giant chased them. Jack rounded a bend, gravel sliding beneath his feet.

"Down there!" Ruby cried, pointing to a small ledge below the path. Danny jumped first, his arms windmilling to keep his balance as he landed on it. Ruby went next, falling into a light-footed crouch beside him. Jack sized up the jump, took a deep breath and leapt, adrenaline flooding his veins. He landed and scrambled up on to another narrow path.

The thud of heavy footsteps faded away above them. *We fooled it!* Jack thought, relieved.

BOOM!

Jack staggered as the path bucked and the massive ogre landed just a few yards behind him. *It jumped!* The creature bellowed angrily as the three friends quickly fled further along the ledge. They veered around a hairpin bend and skidded to a halt. In front of them, a rickety wooden bridge spanned a dizzying drop. Ice-blue water tumbled over jagged rocks far below. On the other side of the bridge, a sloping mountain path beckoned. Jack gasped for breath. The thud of the ogre's footsteps rattled his bones and sent pebbles falling from the mountainside above them.

"If the giant reaches the bridge while we're on it, he'll smash it apart," Danny said.

"The river might break our fall,"

Jack said hopefully.

"But those massive rocks won't!" Ruby said.

Jack's stomach squeezed with fear. Back up the path, the vast stone monster filled his view, orange eyes blazing.

"I guess we have no choice," Jack said.

"Let's go!" cried Ruby, sprinting over the bridge, the weathered planks swaying beneath her.

"Come on!" Danny cried, running after her. Jack followed, feeling the wood creak beneath his feet. He kept his eyes on the rocky slope of the far

bank, willing his friends to reach it,
pushing himself faster ...

The bridge gave a tremendous,
terrifying judder.

Jack's heart skipped a beat as he
fell sideways, into the ropes. The
bridge rocked wildly, sending him

tipping out over the gorge. He grabbed
hold of the rope guardrail, hanging
out over the churning rapids that
crashed and foamed below. Danny
had dropped to a crouch in the centre
of the bridge. Up ahead, Ruby gripped
the ropes, knuckles white, staring

back. Her amber eyes flashed and two jets of flame sizzled past Jack. They slammed into the cliff side above the giant. For a moment, Jack thought that Ruby had missed, but then he realised what she was up to. Small stones tumbled down from above, rattling off the monster's head. Then larger stones and then a wave of boulders fell from the rock face.

"Nice shot!" Jack cried. But then, a deafening rumble filled the air as an avalanche crashed down on to the narrow path, burying the ogre, then spilling on to the bridge.

"A bit too good a shot!" Danny yelled

over the roar from the collapsing cliff.

"Hold on!" Jack cried, tightening his grip as the ropes holding up the far end of the bridge were snapped by the crumbling mountainside. The world tipped around him as that end of the bridge plunged downward in an arc. Wind snatched the breath from Jack's throat and his stomach shot into his mouth. He was whooshing backwards and downwards, gripping the dangling rope with his hands ...

CHAPTER 2

MOUNT RAZOR SCHOOL

WITH ONE end of the rope bridge destroyed, it swung to hit the cliff side on the opposite side of the abyss. The collision jolted Jack's whole body.

"Help!" Danny cried, tumbling down towards Jack. Kicking out from the cliff, Jack reached to grab Danny's wrist as he fell past.

"Thanks!" Danny said weakly, boots dangling over the gorge, his face as grey as ash.

"Don't mention it," Jack said. He used his super-strength to haul Danny upwards so he could catch hold of what remained of the destroyed bridge.

Above, Ruby was already climbing upwards, using the planks like the rungs of a ladder. "You OK?" Jack asked Danny. Danny nodded shakily, and set off after her.

Finally, Jack pulled himself up on to the dusty path. He collapsed beside his friends.

"Attention!" a curt voice called from above them. A moment later a tall boy wearing gleaming armour bearing a square tower sigil slid down the slope towards them. "To your feet, soldiers!" he snapped. Two other armoured figures leapt down to join him, both girls with cropped hair and cold stares. More figures followed, until a dozen soldiers stood watching with cool disapproval as Jack, Danny and Ruby scrambled to their feet.

"I'm Matthias," the tall, dark-haired boy at the front of the group told them. He looked a couple of years older than Jack. "I'm head boy at Mount

Razor School. I'm here to show you the way, and to stop you getting into trouble — though it looks like I'm too late for that."

Matthias curled his lip as he eyed the avalanche and broken bridge. Then he took a slender horn from a pouch at his waist and blew a long, low note. As the sound echoed around the canyon, Jack saw the pile of rubble stir. Rocks tumbled away, revealing the crumpled form of the stone giant. The creature slowly unbent, then shook its head, as if to clear its thoughts. Finally, it called out with a long note, very like the blast from the horn, but with a kind of grumpy edge to it.

Matthias blew another series of low blasts. The stone giant rolled its orange eyes, tossed its great hands upwards, then ambled slowly away.

Matthias turned back to Jack and the others, his dark eyes narrowed. "Jotun are unique to this area," he said. "We in the Legion are sworn to protect them. Lucky for you that he wasn't injured."

Danny gaped. "We're lucky we didn't injure him? He attacked us! We almost ended up in the gorge."

"I can see that," Matthias said, frowning. "That bridge won't be easy to fix. What did you do to him anyway? Jotun are normally very peaceful creatures."

Danny flushed. "I might have aimed a sonic blast at him," he admitted. "But only because we thought he was a pile of rocks."

Matthias tutted. "You Heroes and your powers," he said, turning away. "Nothing but trouble ..."

Jack clenched his teeth. But as he

opened his mouth to argue, Ruby
nudged him in the ribs.

Matthias put two fingers to his lips
and let out a long whistle. A strange
keening sound came from high up on
the mountain, like the cry of an eagle
but louder. Clouds of dust billowed up
as a group of animals bounded over a
rocky ledge and sped down the path
towards them. They had the lithe
golden bodies of mountain lions, but
the feathered heads of eagles. Muscles
bulged beneath their sleek coats, and
their curved beaks looked as if they
could tear through a man's chest.
Jack reached for Blaze, his sunsteel

sword. But the Mount Razor students looked unfazed, and the strange animals stopped in front of them. The creatures bowed their heads.

Jack let his hand fall from the hilt of his sword and took a deep breath. *This place is going to take some getting used to ...*

"What are they?" Ruby asked.

Matthias smiled. "Accifaxes. You'll need to cling on tight." The squadron swung up on to the accifaxes' backs.

Danny shot Jack a look of alarm. "Are we seriously going to do this?" he asked. "I'd rather have Olly fly me there than get on one of those things."

"It looks like it's that or be left behind," Jack said. He stepped gingerly towards one of the remaining beasts, noticing its warm, musky smell. The accifax cocked its head, watching Jack with an amber eye.

"You don't mind if I climb up?" Jack asked. Then he gripped the creature's ruff, and leapt up on to its back.

The accifax sped away so fast, Jack felt like his stomach had been left behind. He clung tight as the creature sprang from ledge to ledge without breaking its stride. Risking a glance back over his shoulder, Jack saw Danny and Ruby close on his tail. Danny had his eyes scrunched closed, but Ruby was grinning.

"What a ride!" she cried. The accifaxes bounded up sheer slopes, leapt across crevasses and raced over rocky plains, going way faster than any hoverboard. Jack found himself grinning too. Even Danny seemed to relax, his eyes shining as they arrived in a narrow, rocky canyon.

Matthias and his squadron stood waiting for them in the shadow of a towering cliff. A pair of huge stone doors stood open in the rock face, leading to a torchlit passage beyond. At a signal from Matthias, his crew swung from their mounts and filed through the doorway, quickly disappearing into shadow. Matthias beckoned for Jack, Ruby and Danny to follow him.

Jack could hear the clash of steel

and distant shouts coming from
inside the mountain. They arrived
at an archway and Jack stopped,
staring in awe. A vast cavern spread
before him, containing what looked
like a whole medieval town. At the
centre was a turreted castle, complete
with inky moat. Legionaries, many
around Jack's age and all wearing the
same burnished armour as Matthias
and his crew, hurried between low
stone buildings or sparred in open
courtyards lit by fire pits. Faint
beams of sunlight slanted down from
narrow cracks in the rock far above.

Matthias led Jack, Ruby and

Danny inside, heading between a pair of rectangular buildings. From the savoury smell of stew, Jack figured they must be dining halls. They passed living quarters, weapons stores and a smithy, and eventually reached the gatehouse that spanned the moat of the castle keep. Matthias knocked on the door.

"Enter," said a stern voice.

A wooden desk dominated the firelit room. Red and gold tapestries embroidered with the square tower sigil hung on the walls. Behind the desk sat a tall, powerfully built woman with hawk-like features and

short, greying blonde hair. She looked
up as the students entered, then
nodded to Matthias, who saluted and
then left.

Jack waited side by side with
his friends, while the woman rose
and crossed the room. She circled
them, frowning as she inspected
them. Jack felt himself growing hot
under her gaze.

"I am Commandant Eckles," the
woman said. "You will address me
always by my title. While you are
here, we shall teach you to fight."

"We can fight already, thanks,"
Ruby said, spinning the mirror shield

on her arm. "We are Heroes, after all."

Commandant Eckles sighed.

"'*We can fight already, thanks, Commandant*'," she repeated. "Maybe I should have been clearer. Here you will learn to fight properly, without relying on technology or special powers. You will be treated as the novices you are. Like all our students, you will need to earn the privilege to carry weapons. Now, leave that shield, and any weapons you have brought with you, on my desk, then report to Captain Jana in the training hall."

What?

Jack couldn't imagine parting with Blaze — the sword felt almost a part of him. But he'd promised Chancellor Rex that while he was here, he'd follow the Legion's ways.

He reluctantly placed Blaze on the polished wood, beside Danny's energy

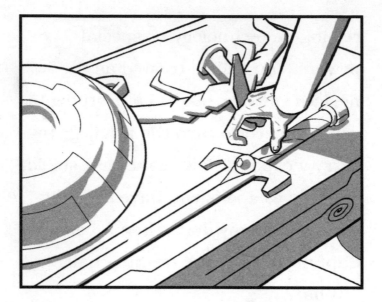

crossbow and Ruby's mirror shield, and he felt his cheeks grow hotter than ever. This trip to the Shardmaw Mountains wasn't what he'd been expecting at all.

CHAPTER 3

UNARMED COMBAT

JACK BLOCKED another right hook with his forearm, then kicked high, aiming for his wiry opponent's chest. Captain Jana sidestepped the kick, her footsteps as light as a cat. The woman kept her gloved hands raised, as if feeling the air for his attack, her eyes hidden behind dark glasses.

"Better," she said, in her cracked old voice. "Still terrible, but better." She relaxed her pose and nodded, signalling an end to the fight.

Jack sagged with relief at the chance to rest. If they'd gone on much longer, he knew she'd have beaten him. Again. And she couldn't even see! He swallowed hard, trying to wet his parched throat. He clearly had a lot still to learn. But after two weeks of near-constant night drills, and agility and endurance training, every muscle in his body ached and his eyes felt gritty from exhaustion.

Several hours each day had been

spent with Captain Jana — Mount Razor School's blind martial arts instructor — learning hand-to-hand combat. *Ironic,* Jack thought, since he was forbidden from using his hands' super strength. A lot of things seemed to be forbidden at Mount Razor, including hot water, soft bedding and any meal that wasn't mutton stew.

Jack crossed to the back of the long, whitewashed training room with its dark wooden ceiling beams, and took a drink of water from a jug on wooden bench. He turned to see how his friends were doing. Ruby and a red-haired boy twice her size were wrestling. Jack could hear them both grunting, but neither seemed to be getting the upper hand.

Nearer to Jack, Danny fought a slender girl with fierce green eyes. They both wore metal gauntlets. Jack knew from experience that those gauntlets packed a punch. Danny panted as he circled his opponent, his fists raised. The girl dived suddenly.

Danny danced back. *Too slow!* Her fist smashed into his chest, sending Danny sprawling. He lay winded, clutching his chest. Captain Jana let out a heavy sigh as she joined them.

Danny scowled. "I get that you don't want us to use our powers. But why can't we use weapons? That's unfair!"

Jana spread her hands. "Life is unfair. How can you expect to use that clumsy crossbow correctly when you can't even use the weapon that is your own body?" Her stern frown softened, and she pulled Danny to his feet. "Our students have practised for years," Jana said. "You're bound to be disheartened at first. But keep it up, and stay focussed. You'll get there."

Jack heard marching feet just outside the training room. He looked up to see Commandant Eckles stride through the door. Matthias and two other armoured students stepped in behind her, each carrying a sack.

"Attention!" Commandant Eckles cried. Ruby and her opponent separated at once. Jack, Danny and Ruby all clicked their heels and saluted as they had been trained.

"Right!" Eckles said, her grey eyes resting on each of them in turn. "I've been listening to your whinging for two weeks now, and I'm sick of it. You think you can fight? Well, prove it!" Eckles held out a hand to one of the students behind her. The student rummaged in his sack and pulled out Ruby's mirror shield.

Eckles took the shield and sent it spinning towards Ruby. "Catch!"

Ruby snatched it from the air. Eckles threw Danny his crossbow, and finally tossed Jack his sword. He caught Blaze by the hilt, grateful for the familiar weight in his hand. Still, an uneasy feeling grew inside him.

What's going on? he wondered.

"They are not ready for this,

Commandant," said Jana. But Eckles waved the remark away.

"Fight!" Eckles cried. Matthias and the two students lifted their swords and lunged forwards.

Jack found himself grinning as he met Matthias's attack. *Sword against sword! This is more like it!* He smashed Matthias's first blow aside and swung a double-handed strike at the boy's chest. Matthias spun out of reach.

"You'll have to be quicker than that!" the boy said. But Jack had expected his move and followed up with a cut to the right. Matthias just managed to dodge the stroke, then leapt back to circle Jack warily. From the corner of his eye, Jack could see Danny keeping his opponent at bay with rubber bolts fired from his crossbow, while Ruby's mirror shield glinted as she slammed it into the third student's chest. *We can do this!*

"Squadron Two! Attack!" Eckles's voice rang out through the hall. Jack heard the clank of armour and clatter of boots, and glanced behind him to see six more fully armed students file through the doorway. The students dived towards them. *Nine against three! Time to regroup.*

"Danny! Ruby! To me!" Jack cried.
He dived past Matthias, striking
a glancing blow to the boy's side,
then sped to the rear of the hall and
vaulted on to the bench there. Danny

and Ruby soon joined him. The three
stood side by side, scanning the
roomful of opponents. Captain Jana
stood with Commandant Eckles by
the door now, her head tipped to one

side as if listening to the fight.

"I'll cover you," Danny cried, lifting his crossbow.

Ruby spun her shield on her arm and smiled. "This should be fun!" The armoured students surged towards them wielding swords and spears. Danny unleashed a barrage of scatter shots. *Clang! Bong! Thud!* Three attackers went down, stunned by the force of the rubber bolts. Jack leapt from the table, meeting two opponents with quickfire swipes. Ruby's shield whistled through the air, slamming into a boy's chest, sending him flying. She leapt down to retrieve the shield.

"Squadron three!" Eckles barked. Jack glanced towards the door. Another dozen or so students filed into the room. Now the whole hall glittered with burnished armour and glinting blades. Jack's guts twisted with fear at the sight. None of the blades looked dulled.

"What's she doing?" Ruby screamed in fury, slamming her shield into the armoured stomach of a hefty, dark-skinned boy. "Is she trying to kill us?"

Jack's sword flashed through the air, blocking a fierce jab from a stern-looking girl with braces. Grunting with effort, he sent the flat of the blade into her chest, throwing her backwards into two more charging students. Commandant Eckles stood watching from the doorway with a fierce, keen look in her eyes.

"We have to use our powers!" said Jack.

"About time!" Ruby said.

"Let's show them what Team Hero can do!" Danny cried. "Engage your ear defenders!"

Jack heard a click through his Oracle's earpiece as Hawk dulled the sounds of battle around him. Danny let out a terrific explosion of sonic force. The Mount Razor students hesitated, and Jack felt a flash of hope, but then they threw their shields before their faces, blocking the worst of Danny's sonic attack.

The girl with braces stabbed for Jack's throat from one side, while Matthias swiped from the other. Jack ducked the girl's blow and met Matthias's sword with his own, using his super strength to smash the blade from Matthias's grip. But even as his sword was wrenched from his fingers, Matthias tugged a dagger from his belt and stabbed up at Jack's belly. Jack twisted away, impressed at the boy's quick thinking, then felt a shock of fear as another blade crashed down towards him from his left. A jet of red flame licked through the air, striking the sword. *Ahhh!* The girl with braces cried out in pain as her sword glowed red hot. *Clang!* The weapon clattered to the ground and Jack shot Ruby a look of thanks. But still more students pushed forward.

This is hopeless! We need to work together ...

"Ruby! Danny!" Jack called. "Time to team up and make some serious noise!" He pointed towards the thick wooden beams that held up the roof. "Are you ready for a lift, Ruby?"

he asked. She grinned at him and
nodded, slinging her shield on to her
back. Jack threw her upwards. She
grabbed the beam and swung up

into a crouch. She lifted her shield.
"Ready!" she called.

Danny let rip, sending a sonic blast
upwards at Ruby's mirror shield.
The sound scattered, reverberating
around the room, growing in volume
as it bounced from the walls. Even
with his ear defenders engaged,
the noise hit Jack like a blow. The
armoured students staggered and fell.
A jug of water exploded, and chunks
of plaster and stone pattered down
from the ceiling. Jack took his chance.
Using the flat of his blade, he knocked
a sword from the nearest student's
grip. Two jets of flame sizzled down

from above, setting alight a wooden shield. The girl that held it yelped and dropped it. Between Jack's sword skill and Ruby's flames, it wasn't long before all the armoured students had been disarmed. They all gave up trying to fight and writhed on the floor, covering their ears.

Danny finally paused for breath, and the room fell silent, but for moans of the Mount Razor students on the floor and the crackle of flames. The training hall was in total ruins.

"I've seen enough!" Commandant Eckles cried from the doorway. "Everyone out! Matthias, Hero

Academy students — you stay."

She does not seem happy, Jack thought, his heart sinking.

Once the room had emptied, Commandant Eckles picked her way across the rubble-strewn floor to stand before them with Matthias.

Jack held his head high as he braced himself for more disapproval from the leader of Mount Razor.

Commandant Eckles shook her head. "I will never approve of how much you Heroes depend on your powers," she began. "Our founder, Wulfstan Hightower himself, would be appalled. He was born with certain

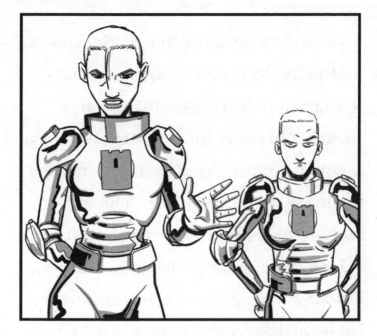

abilities, but it was his skill and discipline that made him the greatest hero of his time. There is no denying your gifts are remarkable. But it's the way you work together that makes you a formidable force."

Jack frowned, confused. "So, you're not going to punish us?" he asked.

Commandant Eckles shook her head. "This was all a test to see if you could combine your abilities with the training we've given you. The only way to be sure was to make you think you were in true danger."

Ruby gasped, "We didn't come here to be attacked. We're supposed to be on the same side."

Eckles spread her hands. "This was not how I hoped to test you, but we've run out of time. I needed to know right away if Rex was correct about the three of you. Thankfully, he was.

You are just what we need."

"For what?" Danny asked, frowning.

"We have a serious problem," Eckles said. "Raina the Vile, one of the Legion's most terrible foes, is returning. She is part human and part dragon, can wield fire, and is a shape-shifter who can take on any form she wishes. Wulfstan himself vanquished her over a thousand years ago, and stripped her of several of her abilities. Much of our knowledge about these powers has been lost over the centuries. However, we do know that one set of Raina's artefacts, the Orbs of Foresight, were secured in a glacial maze not far from here."

"Good thing they're kept safe," Ruby said. "A kid at our school called Olly managed to get hold of a powerful artefact called the Flameguard, and that caused a whole world of trouble."

"Alas, therein lies our problem," Eckles said. "They *were* safe. Until last night. A thief broke into the school's vault and took a scroll containing the password to open the ice maze."

"Well, don't look at us!" Danny said, "We didn't even know it existed!"

Commandant Eckles shook her head. "I am not accusing you. I am *recruiting* you. The maze is no longer secure. I need you to retrieve the Orbs so we can find a safer place for them."

"Sounds simple enough," Jack said.

"If it were simple, I would not have asked for your help," Eckles snapped. "From what our history books say, the maze is heavily fortified and full of traps. Though it pains me to say so, you three Heroes are better equipped to retrieve the Orbs than the Legion, although Matthias will go with you." Eckles unclipped a small lamp from her belt and passed it to Ruby. "You will need this. Once lit, this lantern will protect you from the

maze's traps. Oh — and you must avoid touching the Orbs. The legends suggest that handling them can be ... dangerous." She took a small metal box from her belt pouch and gave it to Jack, "Keep them in this." Eckles's keen grey eyes rested on them each in turn once again. "Soldiers," she said firmly. "This mission must not fail. The fate of the whole world depends on it."

CHAPTER 4

THE ICE MAZE

JACK WATCHED as Ruby stepped
over the lip of the ice cliff far above
him. She leaned back, relying on her
harness for support. This was the
most dangerous part of the descent.
Ruby braced her feet wide and
started shuffling down, feeding the
rope through her hands. When she

finally reached the bottom, she gave a thumbs-up to Danny, who waited at the top of the cliff.

"Your turn!" she called. A moment later, Danny stepped back over the lip of the glacier and abseiled slowly to the bottom.

"OK, Matthias," Danny called up to the young Legionary. "It's your—" He broke off, his eyes widening.

"What's wrong?" Jack asked.

"I heard a thud," Danny said, cocking his head to listen with his bat-like ears. "And what sounded like a yelp. Matthias! Are you OK?" he called.

The three friends stood side by side,

watching and waiting for the dark-haired boy to appear.

Ruby frowned. "What's keeping him?"

A pale face appeared at the top of the glacier, framed by a thick fur hood — unlike the Team Hero students, Matthias didn't have a temperature-controlled bodysuit to keep him warm. "I'm fine," Matthias answered. "Why wouldn't I be?" Then he turned and hopped backwards off the cliff face, bouncing down the vertical glacier, until he made one final huge leap near the bottom, landing neatly on both feet.

"Now let's go and find those Orbs," Matthias said, grinning. "If you bunch of weaklings aren't thinking of wussing out already, that is."

Ruby raised an eyebrow. "No — I think we're good to go, thanks," she said. "And if this is what you're going be like out of the teachers' earshot, I think I preferred you back at Mount Razor."

Matthias shrugged. "You don't have to like me, you just have to do what I say," he told her.

Nice, Jack thought. *I wonder if Commandant Eckles knows that her teacher's pet is on a power trip.*

The four students followed the crevasse east as Commandant Eckles had instructed them. It narrowed steadily as they trudged over the hard-packed snow. Soon they spotted a cluster of orange tents ahead. A pair of Legionaries sat beside a small campfire in front of a gracefully carved archway in the glacier. Pale blue light shone from inside.

As the students drew closer, the two armoured men stood to attention.

Matthias pushed ahead of Jack. "I'm the leader, remember!" he said, approaching the guards. "What news?" Matthias asked them.

"The entrance to the maze has been breached," answered a burly man with frost clinging to his beard, "but since we arrived, no one has come out.

There is a good chance the thieves are still inside. Be on your guard."

Matthias tossed his head. "I'm not afraid," he said, marching through the archway into the strange blue light. He turned to look back. "Well? Are you coming or not, scaredy-cats?"

"We need to light the lamp, remember?" Danny called back. He bent over the Legionaries' small campfire, and used a burning twig to light the wick. When he stood, the lamp shone a steady golden light on to the snow and ice around them.

Jack, Ruby and Danny stepped together into the ice tunnel. Once inside, Ruby gasped. "It's beautiful!" she said. Jack gazed about and had to agree. The walls of the carved tunnel shone an azure crystalline colour that seemed to glow from within. Windblown snow on the cavern floor glittered in the torchlight.

The tunnel curved gently as they followed it, so they could never see far ahead. Jack's breath misted the air before him, and the tip of his nose tingled, but he was warm enough inside his suit. Suddenly Matthias stopped dead and scrabbled backwards on the ice. He pointed ahead. Staring back at them from alcoves on either side of the tunnel were two enormous blue wolves. They stood with their backs arched and their fangs bared. Jack's heart skipped a beat, but then he grinned. The wolves weren't moving. They both stood on plinths, gripping the ice with shiny talons made of silvery metal.

"Statues made of ice!" Danny said.

"I knew that," Matthias snapped. Danny rolled his eyes, but followed without comment. More ice wolves stood in alcoves along the length of passage. As Jack passed them, he couldn't help noticing how their cruel, pale eyes seemed to follow him. But after he'd passed half a dozen or so of the huge, snarling statues, he started to get used to them.

They rounded a curve into a cathedral-like room, with frozen

pillars reaching up to the domed
ceiling, and more tunnels leading off
in every direction.

"Ah, here's the maze!" Ruby said.
"Well, this should be simple enough

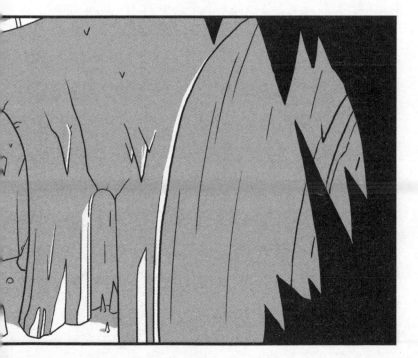

to solve. I'll just melt a way through!"
Ruby focussed her amber eyes on
the wall ahead of them. Two jets of
fire sizzled towards the smooth blue
surface. "Wah!" Ruby leapt aside as
her fire-beams bounced off the wall
and shot straight back towards her.

The streams of fire ricocheted off
a pillar behind them. "Watch out!"
Jack pushed Matthias out of the way,
sending him skidding over on the ice.
Jack dived down beside him. Danny
fell to a crouch, his hands covering
his head, and Ruby threw up her
shield as the fire bounced back and
forth off the ice walls. Once the

flames had fizzled out, the students got to their feet. Matthias rubbed his elbow and eyed Jack darkly.

"I don't get it," Ruby said, confused. "Fire melts ice."

Danny held a hand to his earpiece. "According to Owl, the ice has protective properties that make it resistant to flames."

"I guess that makes sense," Ruby said. "If Raina the Vile can use fire as a weapon, the maze would have been designed to withstand it. Unfortunately, then, that means my powers are pretty useless. Any other ideas?"

"I could use sonar," Danny said. "I'm still not brilliant at it, but I've been practising with Owl. I reckon we can map a path through."

"Go for it," Jack said. "Matthias — I suggest you cover your ears."

Danny turned to the array of passages before them, then started to hum in a loud, low drone. The sound seemed to rise up through Jack's boots and into his body. His vision blurred from the vibrations and then he realised that the ice all around him was quaking from the sound of Danny's voice. Eerie groans and creaks echoed down through the glacier, mingling with Danny's strange song, along with sharp pops and snaps like distant gunfire. *The sound of ice cracking* ... Jack thought with a shudder. Thankfully, Danny's droning came to an abrupt halt. "How was that, Owl?" Danny asked his Oracle. Jack heard a crackle in his ear as his own Oracle synced with Danny's.

"I'm receiving the sound echoes now," Owl said. *"Many of these tunnels are dead ends. Others end in vertical drops that I doubt a human would survive. Only one route leads all the way through. Take the centre*

tunnel ahead, and I'll guide you."

Jack had expected Matthias to object when they explained the plan, but he seemed content to follow them through the maze. "So long as you remember who's in charge!" was all he said. So, with Danny in the lead holding the magical lantern, they followed Owl's directions.

"Keep an eye on that lamp," Jack told Danny as they entered the first tunnel. "The maze is quiet now, but let's make sure it stays that way." The lamp was protecting them from the maze's defences, but Jack couldn't help shuddering at the thought of what traps and other nasty things lurked within these frozen walls.

The first tunnel sloped steeply upwards. Jack and the others slipped several times before they got the hang of walking on the tilting ice. Eventually the passage turned sharply, revealing three more passages. One of them had jagged spikes lining the ceiling and walls.

"Let me guess," Danny said, pointing to the spiked passage. "We're going that way?"

"Correct," Owl answered. Jack pressed the tip of his finger to one of the spikes as he passed. A bead of

blood welled up from the skin. *These things are razor sharp.*

"I'm glad we've got the lantern," Ruby said, shuddering, "or I expect these spikes would be moving."

The route Owl mapped took them through dozens of turns. As they travelled deeper into the glacier, the light shining from the ice became a richer, darker blue. They passed more booby traps — ice blades curved out from the ceiling and floor, fragile lattices of ice crystals covered pits of icy needles, and glittering pulley systems dangled crystalline maces above their heads. But in the steady glow of the lantern, all the traps remained dormant, like a computer game on pause. Eventually, they came to a small chamber with just one tiny, circular exit, which sloped downwards like a slide.

There was no way of seeing what was at the other end of the chute. "I'll go first, and check it's safe," Jack said. "Danny, pass me the lamp."

"OK, but hurry," Danny said. "Some booby trap could go off in here while you're gone."

Jack nodded. He seated himself at the top of the chute, and then gripped the lamp with both hands.

He took a deep breath. *Here goes ...*

Whoosh!

He shot down the tube, gleaming ice whizzing past. A moment later he was thrown from the end of the tube into a rectangular chamber with long spikes jutting down from the ceiling. A single door in the right-hand wall stood open. *That must be the way out of the maze!* Jack scrambled to his feet. A figure ahead moved. Heart racing, Jack's hand fell to the hilt of Blaze. Then he realised the figure was himself. He was staring into a huge ice mirror.

"All good down here!" Jack called up

to his friends. Ruby skidded into the room and stood, quickly followed by Danny and Matthias. Looping words had been carved into the surface of the mirror. *"Reveal Your True Self,"* Jack read.

"Well, I'm here," Danny said, looking at his reflection in the mirror, confused. "And I look the same as I always have."

"Hmmm. Maybe the mirror is to reveal Raina's true identity," Ruby said. "We know she can wield fire, but Eckles also said that she was a shape-shifter."

Jack nodded. "That must be it," he

said. "So now we're through the maze. Shall we—" Jack stopped in shock, staring hard at the features reflected under Matthias's fur hood in the mirror. The face that smirked back at him wasn't Matthias's at all — it was Olly's — Jack's former Hero Academy classmate who'd turned thief and traitor, and who hated Jack with a passion.

"Surprise," said Olly.

CHAPTER 5

WOLF ATTACK

OLLY SHRUGGED off his coat, revealing the Flameguard underneath — a silver breastplate decorated with glowing red swirls that he'd stolen from an ancient vault in the hidden cities of Solus. With a jab of horror, Jack noticed that the magical armour's fiery red lines had crept up Olly's neck and on to his arms.

With an echoing crack the immense ice spikes in the ceiling broke loose and sliced down, straight towards Olly. *The maze must sense Olly's an enemy!* Before Jack could warn him, Olly glided away through the air. The spikes crashed harmlessly on to the floor, shattering into glittering pieces.

"Ha ha!" Olly crowed, using his flying ability to hover a metre from the ground. "I'm way too quick for a trap like that. Thank you all for getting me through the maze. My

mistress told me that once I'd opened
it with the password I'd need help to
solve it. But now I'm here, nothing
will stop me!" Olly spread his arms
and the red streaks on his breastplate
and skin pulsed with light. A bright
red beam shot from the centre of his
chest, straight
towards Jack.
Jack dived out of
the way, but the
bolt of energy
glanced off the
curved back
wall of the cavern
at a crazy angle.

"Get behind me!" Ruby cried, lifting her mirror shield. Danny and Jack dived behind the shield, while Ruby deflected the deadly beam until it eventually fizzled out.

"Olly!" Ruby snapped. "Are you seriously trying to kill us? Look at what you've become — someone who'd steal, and murder his own classmates for power. The Flameguard's taken you over. You have to fight it!"

Olly's broad grin froze, then faded for a moment. For a heartbeat, Jack thought maybe Ruby had got through to him. But then the red tendrils that flowed across the

Flameguard glowed brighter. Olly scowled angrily. "You're just jealous! My mistress has shown me what the Flameguard can do, and it gives me powers you couldn't even imagine. She taught me to use it to change into whatever shape I like!"

"But at what cost?" Jack said, setting the lantern on the ground. "You're being controlled! What did you do with Matthias?"

Olly sneered. "He'll wake up with a little headache, that's all. Now, if you don't mind, I have real hero work to do, restoring my mistress's stolen powers!"

Mistress ... Jack looked at Danny and Ruby. "He's working for Raina!" He brandished Blaze. "If you want to get the Orbs of Foresight, you'll have to come through us first!"

Danny lifted his crossbow, and Ruby's eyes flashed, but Olly's grin only broadened.

"Not necessary," he said. His breastplate glowed bright, and another bolt of red light shot from his chest. The red beam struck the magical lantern Jack had set down on the ice, shattering it.

No!

A moment later, ominous clunks

and grating whirrs echoed from the maze behind them as the labyrinth's booby traps came to life.

"The maze will take care of you!" Olly said. "I just need to get the Orbs and go." He swooped towards the chamber door.

Jack dived after him, half-skidding, half-running over the slippery ground. He burst from the chamber with Ruby and Danny right behind him, arriving in a vast, shadowy cavern. A slender, translucent bridge spanned a deep fissure, leading to an archway in a great glacial wall. Amber light spilled through from

the doorway. *That must be where the Orbs of Foresight are kept!* Jack realised. Olly was already flying over the bridge. Jack raced after him, arms spread as his feet slipped on the ice. *If only I could fly like Olly!*

Suddenly a long low growl echoed from behind them, sending a shock of fear down Jack's spine. He lurched to a stop and turned.

"Why am I not at all surprised?" Danny said.

Jack swallowed hard. Half a dozen giant ice wolves stood crouched before them, ready to attack. With the lantern extinguished, the statues they'd passed on their way into the maze had come alive! Their pale eyes blazed with a hungry light and their curved fangs glinted.

Twin blasts of fire jetted from Ruby's eyes towards the ice beasts, hitting the lead wolf square in the chest. *Fizz!* The fire beams ricocheted off. The ice wolf snarled but stood its ground. Ruby's flames left no mark.

"They must be made of the same magical ice as the maze!" Ruby said in dismay.

"I've got this!" Danny said. He let out a roar, blasting the wolf pack with a wall of sound. The wolves tensed, their ears flicked back and their glowing eyes narrowed. Jack felt the ice beneath his feet quake.

A huge chunk splintered from the ceiling and came crashing down amongst the wolves, bursting into fragments. Ruby threw up her shield to protect them as more ice crashed down around them.

"Yikes," Danny said. "Too risky to try that again! We'll bring the whole glacier down on us!"

With a chorus of furious snarls, the ice wolves charged. Jack drew back his sword, and Danny fired his crossbow. *Thwack!* One wolf shot sideways, a metal bolt embedded in its chest. *Crack!* Another wolf hit the ice, a bolt blowing off a chunk of its shoulder. Four wolves still hurtled forwards, and the fallen ones were already rising to rejoin the pack.

Jack tightened his grip on Blaze and leapt forwards to meet the lead wolf, slashing his blade across the creature's snout.

From the corner of his eye he saw Ruby slam her shield into another wolf's flank. The force of the blow sent her skidding backwards. Danny fired shot after shot. Snarling jaws snapped towards Jack. He smashed them aside with a double-handed blow from Blaze. He glanced to see Ruby cowering before a gigantic ice

wolf, her shield raised. The wolf let out a strangled yelp, flung sideways by one of Danny's metal bolts.

Ruby scrambled up, her shield poised, as more wolves leapt her way. "There are too many of them!" she cried. Jack's sword slashed and hacked at gleaming hides. Ruby's shield batted aside slashing metal claws. Danny used his crossbow as a club, beating the creatures around the head. But the wolves were relentless. Jack kept his weight low as he fought, his feet spread wide for balance, but with each strike and turn he slipped just enough to make his blows clumsy.

Jack's mind raced to think of a plan. The wolves didn't bleed and superpowers seemed to have almost no effect on them. And on top of that, with their sharp metal claws, they had no trouble keeping their footing on the ice. *That's it!* Jack realised. "Danny! Ruby!" he cried. "Go after the wolves' claws. They use them to grip the ice!"

Ruby grunted and sent the edge of her shield crashing into an ice wolf's snapping jaws. Then, frowning hard, she focussed her eyes at its paws and shot two white-hot beams of fire.

The claws began to melt. The wolf let out a snarl of rage and sprang. Ruby leapt aside. The wolf landed right where she'd been standing. Its icy paws skidded on the frozen ground as it scrambled for grip.

"It works!" Ruby said, firing twin beams at another wolf's paws.

BOOM! One of Danny's fire-bolts slammed into a wolf's paws and exploded into flames. The wolf shot straight up in the air like a startled cat, leaving shiny drops of molten metal on the ground.

Jack ran as fast as he could over the slippery ice, towards the yawning crevasse. From behind him he could hear booms and sizzles alongside angry growls. He skidded to a stop at the lip of the crevasse and turned. He smashed his sword against the ice, making the cavern echo. "Come and get me!" shouted Jack. The wolves' muzzles went up. They howled, baring their ice teeth. All at once, the pack broke into a run, heads lowered and hackles raised, straight towards him.

This had better work! Jack thought.

CHAPTER 6

THE ORBS OF FORESIGHT

JACK CROUCHED, standing his ground, waiting for just the right moment. When the first wolf drew so close Jack could see the gleam of his sword reflected in the beast's sheeny hide, he threw himself sideways. He turned to see the six wolves scrabbling frantically, but without their metal claws they couldn't stop themselves from flying over the sheer drop, into the icy pit. The echoes of their howls faded as they vanished into darkness.

"Haha!" Danny punched the air. "Nice work, guys!"

Ruby grinned and spun the shield on her arm. "Easy peasy!"

Jack let out a shaky breath and got to his feet. "Now all we have to do is stop Olly," he said. "Let's go."

Jack hurried across the narrow bridge with his eyes fixed on the glowing doorway. He stepped through the archway into a brightly lit chamber dominated by the towering ice statue of an armour-clad warrior. Olly stood at the foot of the statue holding a pair of glowing orange jewels in one hand. He was eerily still, as if in some kind of trance.

"What's up with him?" Ruby asked.

"He touched the Orbs," Jack said. "Commandant Eckles said not to."

Jack pulled the small metal box Eckles had given him from his top pocket, dashed over to Olly and used the box to scoop the Orbs from his palm. Olly shook his head and blinked as if coming out of a dream. His forehead creased as he stared at his empty hand. Then he looked up at Jack. Olly's puzzled frown changed into a scowl of hatred.

"Give those back!" he cried, reaching for the orange Orbs. "They belong to my mistress." Jack shoved the box into his pocket, then lifted his sword.

"Not a chance!" he said.

"Then I'll have to take them by force!" Olly snarled.

"You just try it!"

The swirling red lines on the Flameguard flared bright. An idea formed in Jack's mind. He thought of what he'd learned at Mount Razor. *Sometimes superpowers can do more harm than good.*

ZAP! A glowing beam shot from Olly's chest. Jack leapt aside, dodging the beam. It flashed past him, hit the

ice chamber's wall and rebounded straight towards Olly. Red energy exploded against Olly's Flameguard with a flash, throwing the boy backwards through the air. *CRACK!* As Olly slammed into the far wall, the ice wall of the cavern shattered in a glittering cascade and bright sunlight flooded the room. The rubble tumbled into an icy abyss, and beyond, a vista of mountains spread under a blue sky. "It's the other side of the glacier!" exclaimed Jack.

Knocked unconscious, Olly was skidding towards the edge of the drop.

"Olly!" Jack cried. He broke into a

run, then threw himself forwards, landing on his stomach, and grabbed Olly by the foot as he slid over the edge. But as he did so, the Orbs of Foresight shot from their box in his top pocket and tumbled into the chasm. Jack snatched one from the air with his free hand. Immediately, it felt like something exploded in his brain, filling his whole world with bright orange light. A vision formed in his mind — a tall, stern-looking man, wearing golden armour, his sword lifted against an armoured creature coiled before him. The creature had the head and arms of a dark-haired

woman, but the body and tail of a slender lizard. *It must be Raina!*

"You shall trouble this world no

more, Raina!" the warrior cried.

The dragon woman let out a hideous cackle. "Perhaps," she said, "but I foresee that the world will soon face a far greater danger than me. Power corrupts, doesn't it, Wulfstan? And as you keep saying, there is no one more powerful than you."

Wulfstan gritted his teeth and glared at Raina, his eyes suddenly glowing red. Then he drew back his sword and lunged. With another flash of orange light, the vision vanished.

Jack found himself staring down into the crevasse with one hand gripping Olly's foot and the other

Raina's jewel. He realised that Danny and Ruby were each clinging to one of his legs, keeping him from falling. He searched for the second Orb, and spotted it glowing brightly on a lip of ice far below. Suddenly, a hooded figure dashed out from beneath an overhang, snatched up the Orb and hurried away into the shadows.

"Someone's down there!" Jack cried, "They stole the other Orb!"

"Not much we can do about that now," Ruby said, her teeth clenched from supporting Jack and Olly's weight. Ruby and Danny heaved at Jack's legs, pulling him up, and Olly with him. They lay on the ice, heaving in gasps of air.

"Hey, do you need help?" a woman's voice echoed from above. Armoured Legionaries with ropes and climbing gear gazed down at them from the top of the glacier far above.

"Yes, please!" Jack shouted back. He checked Olly's breathing and pulse.

"He'll be fine," Ruby said. "I expect he'll have a headache for about a week, but I'm sure he'll recover."

"I wouldn't want to be him when he does," Danny said. "Chancellor Rex is going to eat him alive! Not to mention Commandant Eckles."

"I've a feeling Commandant Eckles might be too busy to bother about Olly," Jack said. "Raina the Vile has returned, and, as the Commandant said, the fate of the world depends on us making sure she doesn't reclaim her powers." Jack thought of the hooded figure he'd seen take the fallen Orb, and a powerful wave of dread hit him. *Was that her? Was it Raina?*

But then he looked at his friends. Their suits were grubby and their hair mussed up. Ruby had a bruise on the side of her face, and Danny had cuts on his arms. But their eyes

were bright and determined. Jack
grinned. Whatever trouble Raina had
planned, Jack knew Team Hero would
do everything they could to stop her.

AN OFFICIAL MESSAGE
from
HIGHTOWER LEGION

HIGHTOWER

HIGHTOWER

Greetings Cadet,

Congratulations on
your acceptance to Mount
Razor School, the most
elite academy for combat
training in the world.

Should you succeed in your studies here, you will join the most prestigious and honorable of organisations – the Hightower Legion. Our founding harks back a thousand years to the glorious days of Wulfstan Hightower himself, the greatest warrior who ever lived. With his tremendous strength, he defeated heinous villains such as Raina the Vile, and built towering fortresses that even today stand as solidly as the mountains.

While someone of weaker character might be content with being the strongest person in the world, Wulfstan always pushed himself harder. He became a swordsman without parallel, a brawler with an unmatched technique, and a battle strategist without peer. These triumphs were not due to his unusual strength but in spite of them. He taught us that relying on super abilities of any kind is a shameful weakness.

This is the legacy that Mount Razor instills in its students. Unlike other, inferior schools, we forbid the use of powers. Indeed, we are proud that our ideal student has no abilities beyond the excellent mastery of their own bodies and minds. This is the essence of our legendary school.

A thousand years ago, the world was turned upside-down when Wulfstan Hightower disappeared just before the Great Noxx War. To this day, none are sure of what

befell our magnificent founder.
But some of us hold out hope that
Wulfstan will one day return here
to Shadowmaw Mountains, the heart
of the Legion that he founded. If
he does return, I believe he will be
proud of the brave and exemplary
work the Legion has done in his
name.

In time, if you prove worthy, you too
shall contribute to the greatness of
his legacy.

Honour and Strength!

Branwella Eckles

Commandant Branwella Eckles

Headmistress

Mount Razor School

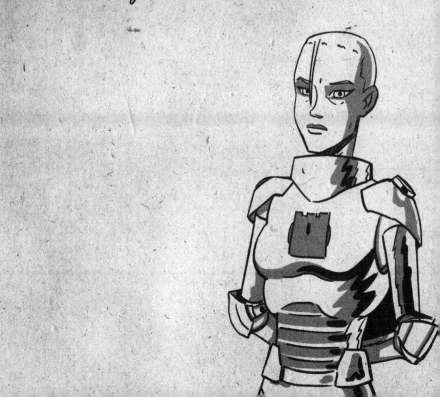

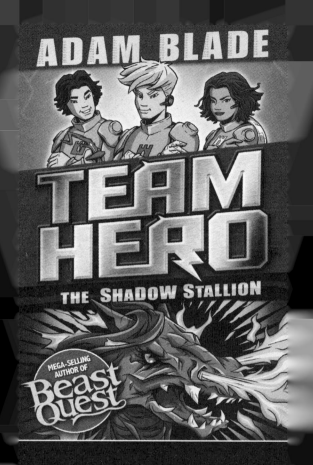

ADAM BLADE

TEAM HERO

THE SHADOW STALLION

MEGA-SELLING AUTHOR OF Beast Quest

READ ON FOR A SNEAK
PEEK AT THE NEXT BOOK

THE SHADOW STALLION

CHAPTER 1

THE JOUST

JACK TRIED to lead the accifax by its reins, but the creature tossed her giant feathered head and let out an angry squawk.

"Easy, Flinta!" said Jack, backing off. Even though he was in full armour, he didn't fancy his chances against a hooked beak that was longer than his arm.

Some of the Legionaries assembled in the tiered stands of the jousting hall laughed, and Jack felt his cheeks burn inside his helmet. *They still think the students of Team Hero are no match for those of Mount Razor.*

"You need to be more assertive," said Captain Jana. "An accifax won't respect you unless you seem in control."

Jack looked towards the Legionary Captain standing with Danny and Ruby, wearing her dark sunglasses. Though she was blind, Jack knew her fighting senses were battle-honed like those of all the teachers here at Mount Razor. None of the students here had special powers like those at Hero Academy, but they prided themselves on being a well-drilled army nonetheless. The school had been here as long as the Academy, hidden way from the rest of the world in the Shardmaw Mountains.

Jack turned back to the huge steed in front of him. Until recently, he'd never have believed such a creature could exist. Flinta had the body of a mountain lion, covered in coarse fur, with claws the size of daggers. But at the accifax's neck, the fur gave way to tawny feathers, and the creature's head was that of an eagle, with large black eyes. Flinta had been easy to handle for the first few rounds of the tournament, but as the day wore on, her mood had become worse.

"Go on, Jack!" said Ruby. "We know you can do it."

"Show it who's boss," said Danny.

"*It* is a *she*," Captain Jana reminded them.

Jack gripped the reins again, and slipped a foot into the stirrup. He felt Flinta buck a little, but used the power in his glowing golden hands to hold on, then hoisted himself into the worn leather saddle.

"A promising start, Hero," said a voice. Matthias bounded past on his own accifax, armour clanking, before turning to call out again. "I wouldn't get too comfy up there, though."

Jack watched the young Legionary canter to the end of the jousting lists, where he seized a lance from a rack. The Hightower Legion shunned the tech of the modern world. The school looked like something from medieval times, with battlements and courtyards and old-fashioned weapons. The vaulted hall they were in had tapestries hanging from the

stone walls, and torches blazing in
sconces at regular intervals.

Captain
Jana brought
Jack his lance
and a battered
rectangular
shield. Jack
hooked an arm
through the
handles then
gripped the
reins again,
and hefted

the lance easily in his other hand.
He squeezed his knees, and Flinta

jerked into motion, springing nimbly to the opposite end of the jousting ground. The crowd began to clap and roar Matthias's name. Jack could see Danny and Ruby cheering him on, but their voices were well and truly drowned out. Both of Jack's friends had been knocked out of the tournament earlier by the more experienced jousters of the Legion. Jack thought perhaps he'd been lucky winning all his rounds so far, even though Jana said he was a natural.

When he was in position, the Captain raised her arm for silence, and the crowd obeyed.

"Welcome, all, to the final joust of the Founder's Day competition!" cried Jana. "The mighty Wulfstan Hightower is looking on in spirit, so make him proud. Matthias and Jack, are you ready?"

Jack nodded and slid down his visor. The world reduced to its narrow opening, and he fixed his stare on his opponent.

"Engage!" shouted Captain Jana.

Jack leant forward and squeezed his knees, driving Flinta into a trot that quickly became a bounding gallop. He watched Matthias charging from the other direction, picking up speed as well. Jack tried to stay calm, as Jana had taught him, focusing his gaze on the point of his lance. The key was not to have any doubts — to charge headlong even though your mind told you it was a *bad, bad* idea. Along the lists, the crowd were just a blur, their roaring voices indistinct. Jack gripped the lance tight, keeping it steady as they closed.

He saw the tip of Matthias's lance come at him, and angled his shield. The point slid past, then ...

SMASH!

The force almost lifted Jack from the saddle, but he held the reins firm.

And then Flinta was slowing and the world and its sounds came back into focus. Apart from his own breathing, the entire hall was silent. Everyone's faces were aghast.

Jack brought Flinta round and saw why. Matthias's accifax was riderless,

and the Legionary himself was on the ground, rolling on to his knees and shaking his head.

I did it, thought Jack. *I won!*

He slipped from the saddle, and rushed towards Matthias to check if he was OK. Before he reached him, the Legionary stood up, tugged off his helmet and tossed it aside in disgust. Jack skidded to a stop, ducking as the helmet shot over his head. "Hey!" he cried.

Matthias glared at Jack, and for a moment Jack feared he might actually lash out. But Captain Jana stepped between them and she was accompanied by Commandant Eckles, head of Mount Razor School. She was holding a silver baton. "Congratulations to Jack of Team Hero. You are this year's champion." She held out the baton to him, horizontally, then pressed a small button in the underside. It extended in a smooth motion, becoming a double-pointed spear. Along its shaft were runic engravings. Jack took it, surprised how light it felt, and nodded gratefully. He saw Danny giving him a double thumbs-up.

"It was a fluke," said Jack.

"Those hands of his give him extra strength, remember?" grumbled Matthias.

Commandant Eckles shot him a disapproving glance. "Don't forget, Matthias, that Wulfstan Hightower himself, founder of our Legion, shared the same power." She raised her voice to address the crowd too. "And may I remind you all that our guests from Hero Academy were the ones who saved one of the Orbs of Foresight from Raina's agent, just as Wulfstan once defeated our old enemy." She pointed towards the largest of the tapestries, which showed an armour-clad warrior with the silver spear fighting against a half-dragon, half-woman riding a monstrous horse-like creature made of black smoke. Jack shuddered. When he'd touched the Orb of Foresight, he'd seen that very battle in a terrifying vision.

He just wished he'd managed to save

both of the Orbs. Legends told that
Wulfstan had stripped Raina of her
evil powers, but somehow she was
back, and eager to restore them. Jack
feared that the Orb of Foresight she'd
recovered was just the start.

Commandant Eckles dismissed
the rest of the students, who began
to drift away to their lessons. Jack
watched them go with deep unease.
*How will they fare in a fight against
Raina? I just beat their best, and I'm
new at this ...*

He pushed the thought away as
Matthias came up, looking sheepish.

"Listen, Jack," he said. "You beat me

fair and square. I shouldn't complain."

Jack offered a friendly smile. *No one likes losing.* "It could have happened differently on another day," he said.

"Of course," said Matthias, quickly. "But we have a custom that, as the loser, I am duty bound to offer you a favour of your choice. So ask away."

Jack was taken aback, but an idea immediately

leapt into his head. The Orb of Foresight had shown him the past last time — what if it could show him the future as well?

I might discover Raina's next move.

But the Orb was kept safe under lock and key in the Legion's treasury. The treasury that Matthias and his band guarded.

"Let me touch the Orb of Foresight again," Jack said.

Matthias frowned at the request. "The granting of a favour is a Legion custom, but even that has limits. I don't think Commandant Eckles would approve. However, I will honour your request. Come tonight at midnight to the treasury." He cast a quick glance to where Captain Jana was replacing the lances in their rack, then lowered his voice, adding, "But don't be seen."

● ● ●

At a few minutes before twelve, Jack and his friends sneaked past the Legion's dormitories. Most of the torches on the walls were extinguished, casting the corridors in an eerie blue-grey glow. Their footsteps shuffled on the uneven flagstones and their breath made clouds in the chill air of Mount Razor.

"At least Hero Academy has central heating," grumbled Danny.

Jack wasn't cold himself, but as he crept on, a shiver passed down his spine. He glanced over his shoulder. He kept expecting a robed figure to appear in the shadows, just like the one that had stolen the second Orb of Foresight. Raina was a shape-shifter, and Jack knew there was a chance she was lurking in disguise at Mount Razor, spying under their noses. It would explain how she knew where to find the Orbs of Foresight in the first place. *We can't trust anyone any more,* Jack thought.

They reached the steep steps to the treasury, where Matthias and a fellow student stood holding pikes. They crossed their weapons as Jack and his friends approached, and the girl with Matthias called, "Who's there?"

"It's all right," said Matthias, as Jack stepped into the torchlight. "They're the friends I mentioned." He took the torch from the wall and led them into a low chamber. In a shallow alcove, the remaining Orb of Foresight rested on a wooden plinth. It glowed with a soft yellow light.

"Go on — touch it," said Ruby.

Before Jack stepped up to the

plinth, he slipped the silver spear-baton from his belt and offered it to Matthias. "To say thank you," he said.

Matthias's eyes widened at the gift, and he reached out, only to draw back his hand. "Thank you, Jack, but I can't. Here in the Legion, weapons are earned through victory in battle. Now, be quick. If you're discovered, we're all in trouble."

Jack cleared his mind, reaching out for the Orb. *Tell me where Raina will strike next*, he willed. *Where is she?*

He closed his eyes and let his fingers fall on the Orb's cold surface. At once, he saw mountains, silhouetted

against a stormy sky. The peaks were
impossibly steep and jagged, and from
their midst he saw a yellow glimmer.
Suddenly, the vision zoomed in so
fast he could feel the rush of wind on

his face. The yellow light beckoned him closer and closer, until he saw a figure standing on a mountain ledge. The light was a single yellow eye — the stolen Orb of Foresight — within a hooded face, and he knew at once that it was their deadly enemy.

Jack's blood turned to ice, and he wanted to look away. But the yellow stone held him.

Check out the next book:
THE SHADOW STALLION
to find out what happens next!

IN EVERY BOOK OF TEAM HERO SERIES ONE there is a special Power Token. Collect all four tokens to get an exclusive Team Hero Club pack. The pack contains everything you and your friends need to form your very own Team Hero Club.

FREE TEAM HERO CLUB PACK

MEMBERSHIP CARDS · MEMBERSHIP CERTIFICATE · STICKERS · POWER GAME · BOOKMARKS

Just fill in the form below, send it in with your four tokens and we'll send you your Team Hero Club Pack.

SEND TO: Team Hero Club Pack Offer, Hachette Children's Books, Marketing Department, Carmelite House, 50 Victoria Embankment, London, EC4Y 0DZ.

CLOSING DATE: 31st December 2018

WWW.TEAMHEROBOOKS.CO.UK

Please complete using capital letters *(UK and Republic of Ireland residents only)*

FIRST NAME
SURNAME
DATE OF BIRTH
ADDRESS LINE 1
ADDRESS LINE 2
ADDRESS LINE 3
POSTCODE
PARENT OR GUARDIAN'S EMAIL

I'd like to receive Team Hero email newsletters and information about other great Hachette Children's Group offers (I can unsubscribe at any time)

Terms and conditions apply. For full terms and conditions please go to teamherobooks.co.uk/terms

TEAM HERO Club packs available while stocks last. Terms and conditions apply.

COLLECT ALL OF SERIES THREE!

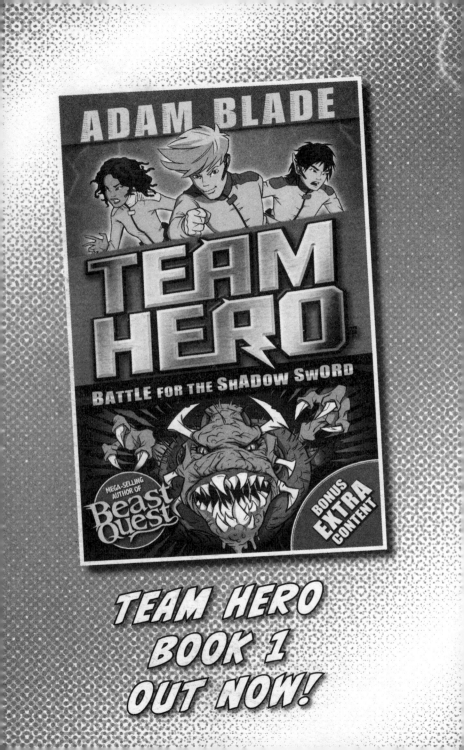

FIND THIS SPECIAL
BUMPER BOOK ON
SHELVES NOW!

READ MORE FROM
ADAM BLADE IN

www.beastquest.co.uk